I NEED MY MONSTER

Written by
Amanda Noll

Illustrated by
Howard McWilliam

Flash
Light
PRESS

Library of Congress
Control Number: 2008934254

ISBN 978-0-9799746-2-5

Editor: Shari Dash Greenspan
Graphic Design: The Virtual Paintbrush

This book was typeset in Kingston,
a font designed by Howard McWilliam.
The illustrations were drawn with pencil on
paper, and painted with digital acrylic paint.

Distributed by Independent Publishers Group

Flashlight Press
527 Empire Blvd. • Brooklyn, NY 11225
www.FlashlightPress.com

Tonight, when I looked
under the bed for my monster,
I found this note instead.

Gone fishing.
Back in a week.
– Gabe

What was I going to do?
I *needed* a monster under my bed.
How was I supposed to get to sleep
if my monster was gone?

I tried to sleep, but it wasn't the same without Gabe.

I missed his ragged breathing.

His nose-whistling.

The scrabbling of his uncut claws.

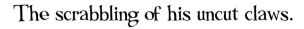

How would I ever get to sleep without Gabe's familiar scary noises and his spooky green ooze?

It was no use. Gabe would be gone for a week and I just *had* to have a monster.

I climbed quietly out of bed so my parents wouldn't hear me.
(Grown-ups have some strange ideas about monsters under beds.)
I knocked on the floorboards, then scrambled back under my covers.
I waited nervously.

Would a new monster appear?
What would he be like?
Would his snorting be as cheerful as Gabe's?

When I heard some creaking under my bed, I knew that the substitute monster had arrived.

"Good evening," said a low, breathy voice. "My name is Herbert and I will be your monster for the evening."

"Herbert? What kind of name is that for a monster?! You don't sound scary at all. Have you ever scared a kid before?"

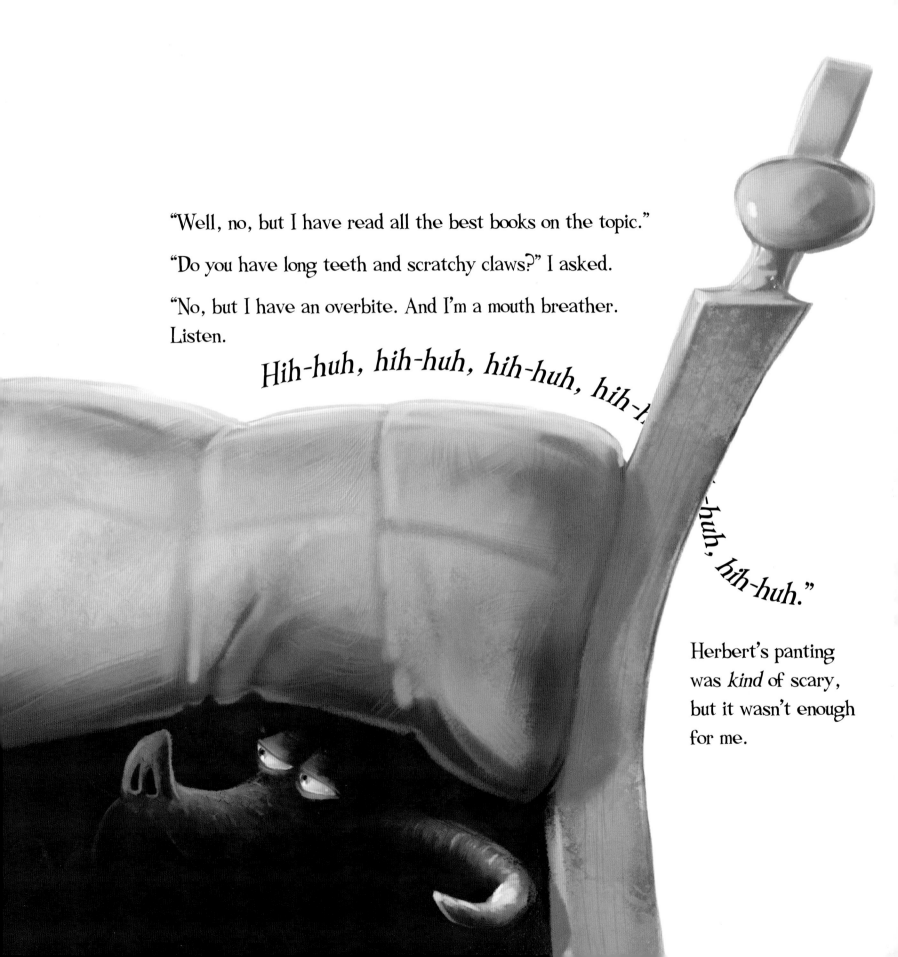

"Well, no, but I have read all the best books on the topic."

"Do you have long teeth and scratchy claws?" I asked.

"No, but I have an overbite. And I'm a mouth breather.
Listen.

Hih-huh, hih-huh, hih-huh, hih-huh, hih-huh."

Herbert's panting
was *kind* of scary,
but it wasn't enough
for me.

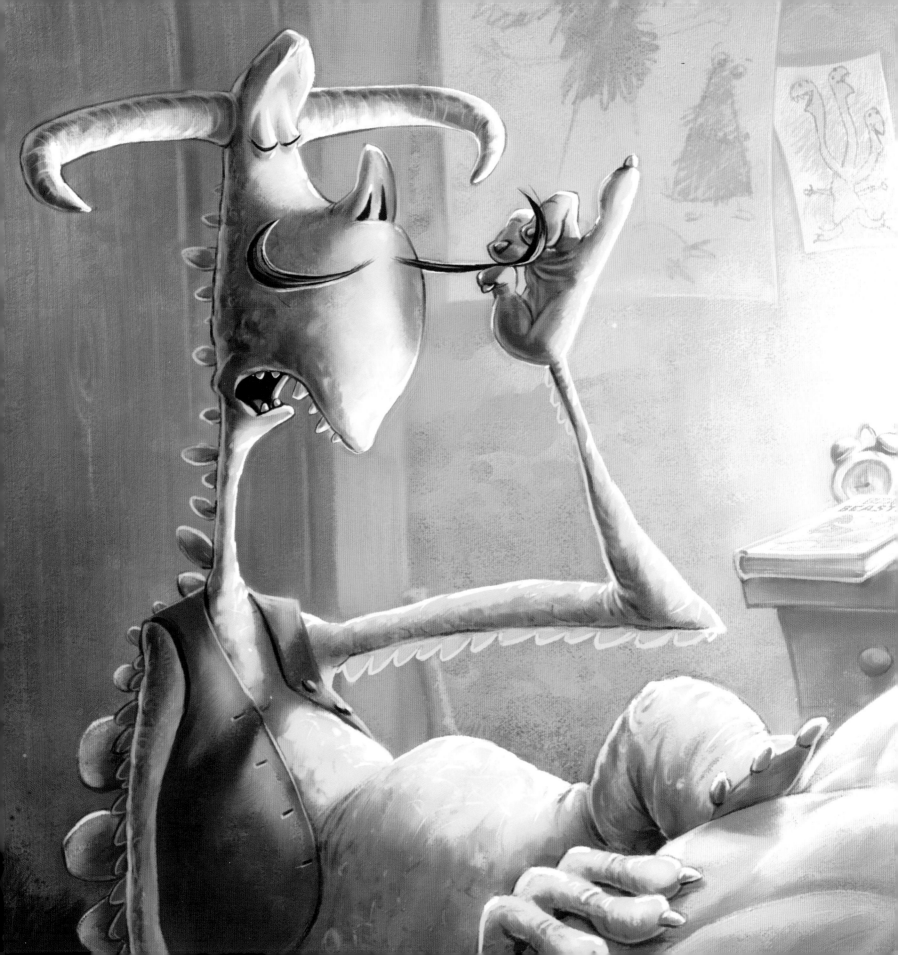

"Listen, Herbert, I'm sorry.
I just don't think this is going
to work. It's nothing personal,
but I really need a monster
with claws."

"Picky, picky," Herbert complained.
"As you wish. I'll go."

There was some more creaking.
Then Herbert was gone.

Some scratching warned me that
a second monster had appeared.

"Good evening," he said in a high, silky voice.
"My name is Ralph. I understand you need
a monster with claws. If you would please
lean over, I will hold out an arm for inspection."

I crouched on the edge of the bed,
hoping to see a horrible shaggy arm
with sharp, ragged nails.

Instead, I was surprised to see sleekly brushed fur with smooth, shiny claws. "Excuse me, I don't mean to be rude," I asked, "but is that nail polish on your claws?"

"Yes, it is," Ralph replied. "I believe professional monsters should always be well-groomed."

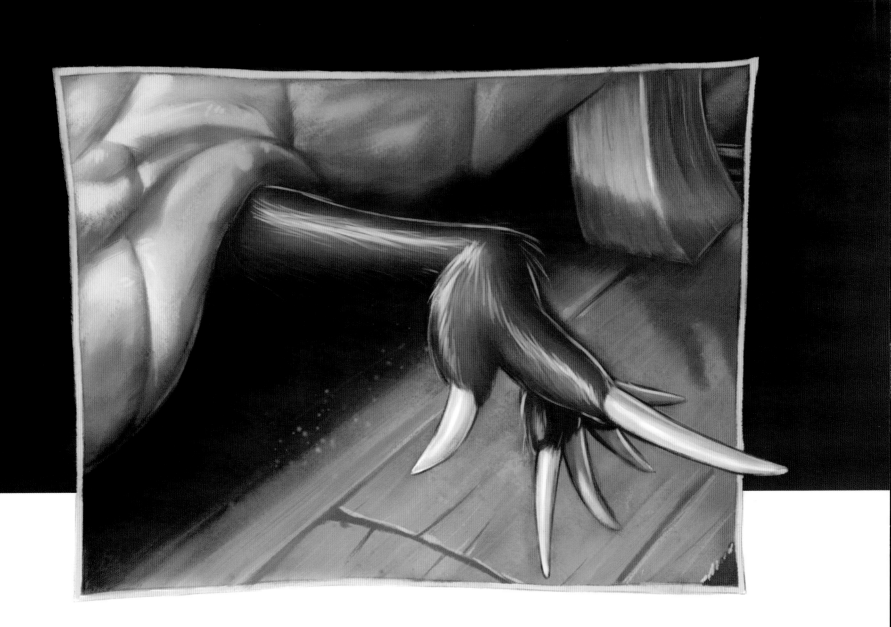

I could tell that this was not going to work either. "I'm sorry to disappoint you, Ralph, but I need a monster with scary claws." *Like Gabe's,* I thought.

I heard some more scratching and I knew Ralph was gone.

A minute later, a third voice from under the bed rasped, "Check out these claws, kid."

I gathered my courage and peered over the edge.

The claws were impressive –
jagged
and dark
and razor-sharp.
So far, so good.
I was a little nervous.

"Could you stick out
your tail?" I whispered.

"Sure.
But don't
get
scared!"

I peeked through my fingers at
the slimy tail slithering over
the foot of my bed.

That's when I noticed the bow.

"Are you a girl monster??"

"Of course I am," she snapped.
"I'm Cynthia. Do you have
a problem with that?"

"Um, yeah, I do," I admitted.
"I definitely need a *boy* monster.
Boy monsters are for boys
and girl monsters are for girls.
Everybody knows that."

"Well, aren't you a picky one,"
she sniffed, and then she
was gone.

Was I being too picky? *NO.*

I knew that my monster needed to be
well-clawed and menacing.

The whole point of having a monster, after all,
was to keep me in bed, imagining all the
scary stuff that could happen if I got out.

Then I heard a shuffling noise. And some slobbering.
A fourth monster was under my bed.
"Hey. The name's Mack."

One look at his claws proved that Mack was a big,
scruffy BOY monster. I shivered. Maybe this one
would work out.

"Those are excellent claws,
but do you have a long tail?"
I leaned over to see.

"No, my tail is stumpy,"
Mack slurped. "But I do have
an unu-u-u-usually lo-o-o-ong...
tongue!"

"Why would I be afraid of
a long tongue?" I asked.

"Oh, I don't know," he said,
trying to sound terrifying.
"You never know when
I-I-I mi-i-i-ight... *lick you!*"

BIZARRE BEASTIES

I fell back on the bed, laughing.

"Well, if you're not even going to try-y-y to work with me..." Mack whined.

I held in my giggles.

"I re-e-e-eally don't think you should send me away," he warned. "Kids who reject five monsters in one night...."

"I did NOT reject five monsters tonight!" I interrupted. "My regular monster went fishing."

"Fishing, eh? Maybe he just left because you're SO-O-O picky. Fine. I'm out of here. But I wouldn't expect another monster tonight if I were you."

How was I ever going to get to sleep
without my monster?

I was surprised to
hear more creaking
under the bed.
Loud creaking.
With scratching.

"I-I thought no more
monsters were going
to appear tonight,"
I said.

"Sorry I'm late, kid."

Whew. It was Gabe.

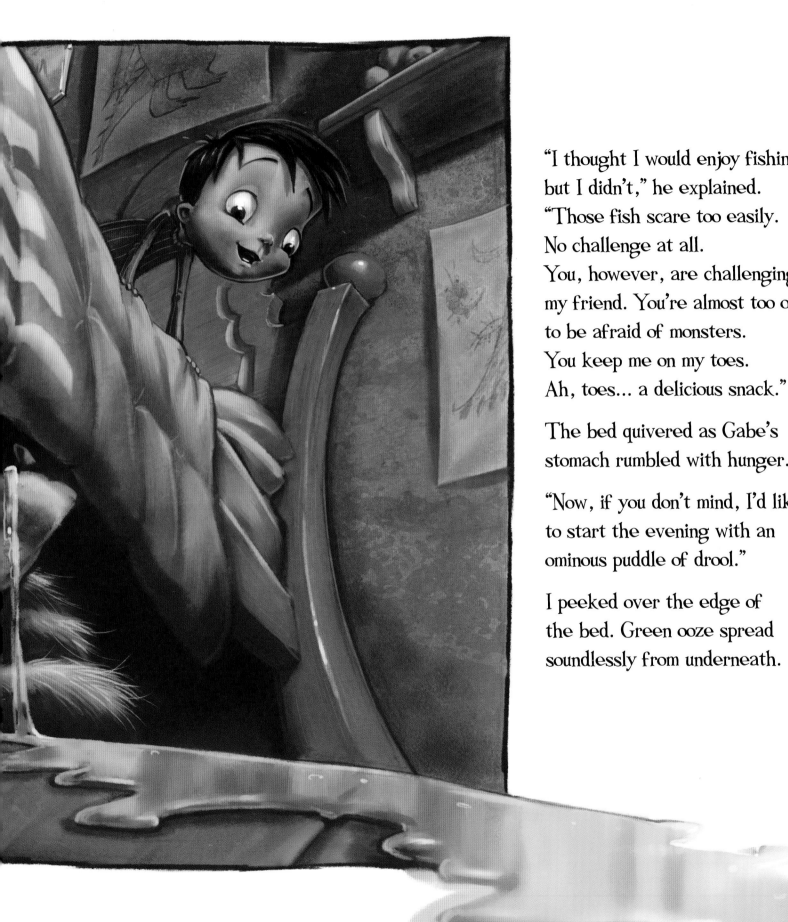

"I thought I would enjoy fishing, but I didn't," he explained. "Those fish scare too easily. No challenge at all. You, however, are challenging, my friend. You're almost too old to be afraid of monsters. You keep me on my toes. Ah, toes... a delicious snack."

The bed quivered as Gabe's stomach rumbled with hunger.

"Now, if you don't mind, I'd like to start the evening with an ominous puddle of drool."

I peeked over the edge of the bed. Green ooze spread soundlessly from underneath.

Then the bed trembled as
Gabe unfurled his spiked tail.
He was daring me to guess
where he might pop up.

I shivered.

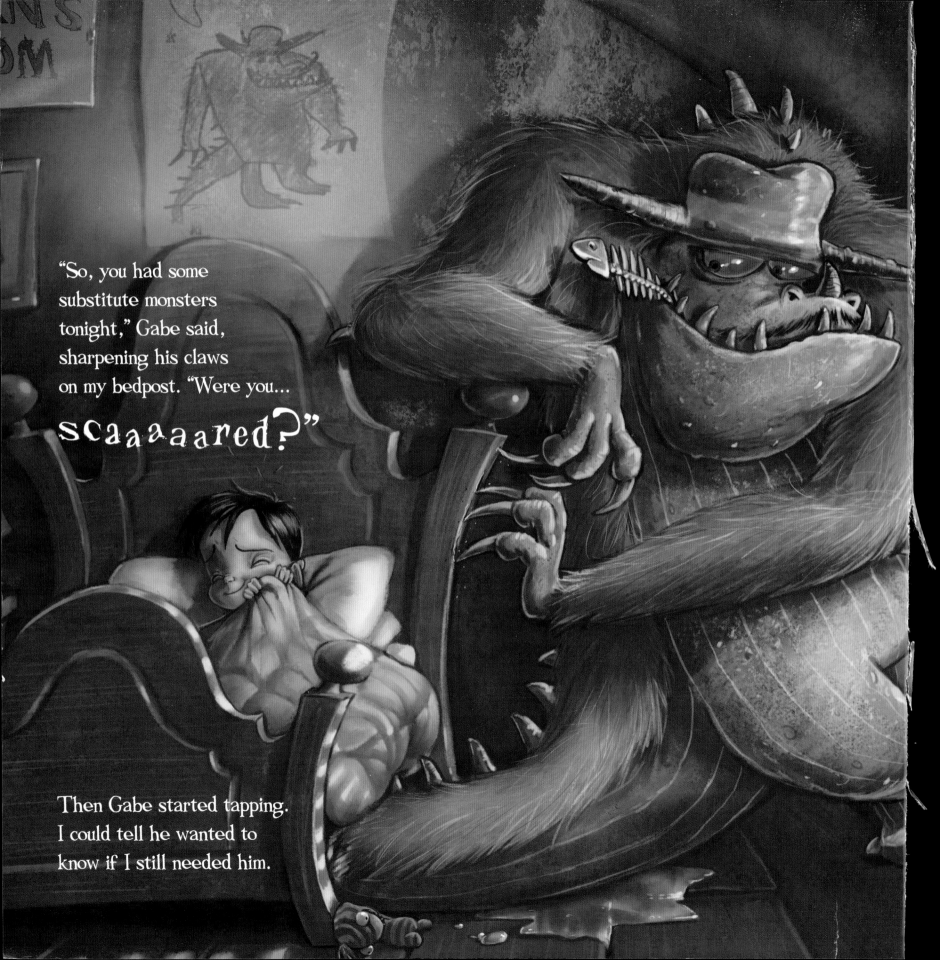

"So, you had some substitute monsters tonight," Gabe said, sharpening his claws on my bedpost. "Were you...

scaaaaared?"

Then Gabe started tapping. I could tell he wanted to know if I still needed him.

"No other monster can scare me like you!" I giggled,
diving under my covers and pulling them up tight.

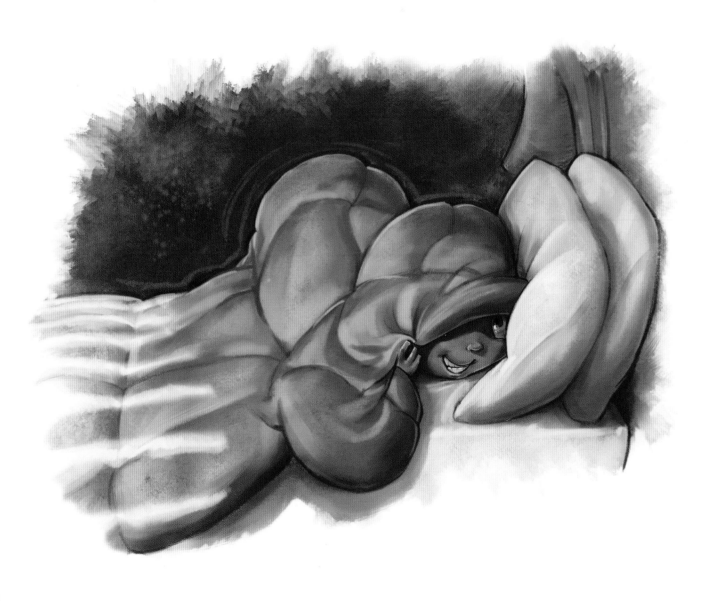

Through the blanket I heard Gabe's soft, comforting snorts.
"Ha! I knew it! We're made for each other," he growled.

When my blanket started to slip off the bed I knew Gabe was ready to eat.
"Now, if you could please stick out your foot," he said, "I'd like to nibble
your pinkie."

I yanked my blanket back up and scrunched my feet in so Gabe couldn't get them.

"No toes tonight, but you can have this," I offered, pushing a pillow off the bed.

I didn't even hear it hit the floor.

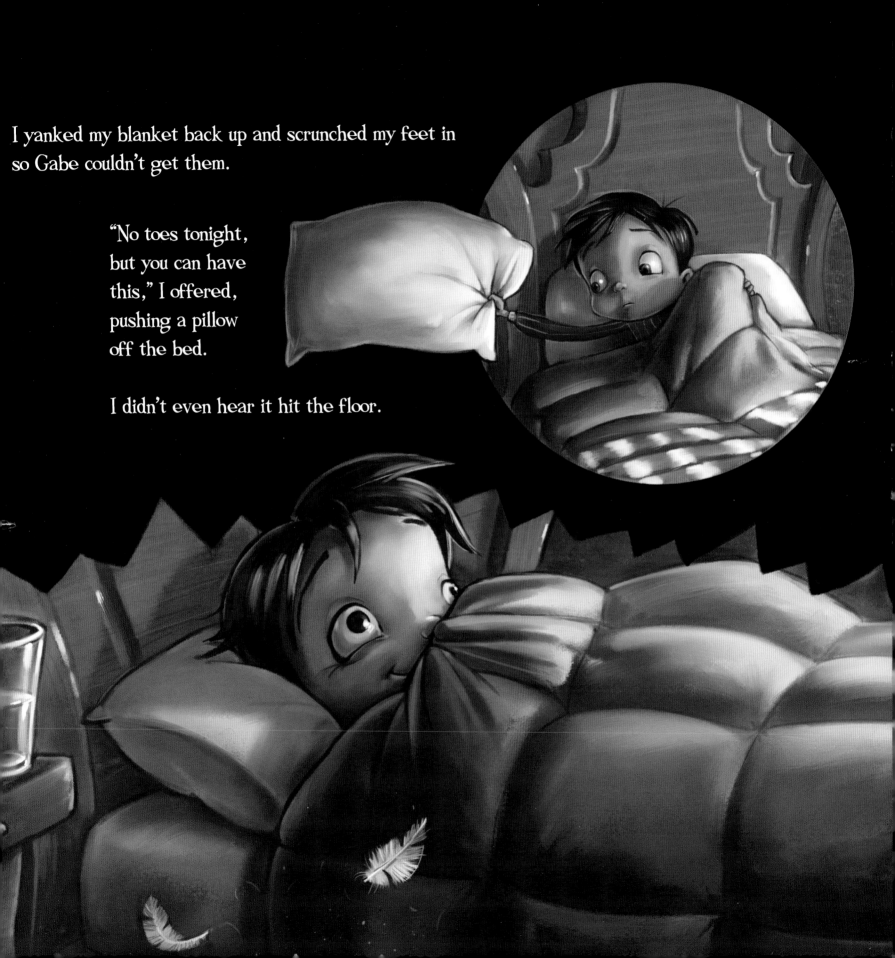

Gabe was back.
The ooze was perfect.
Everything was back to normal.

I shivered again.

I'd be asleep in no time.